T5-DHJ-227

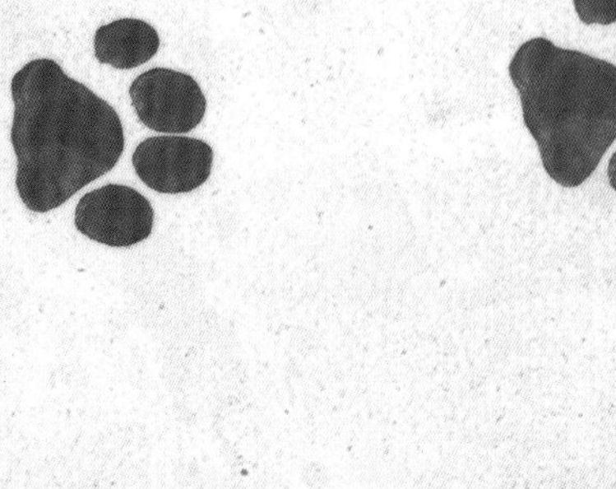

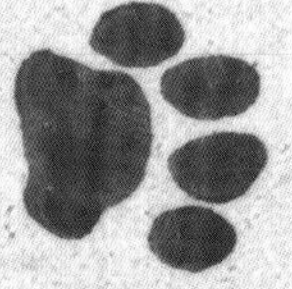

Nelly

The Ponce Inlet Lighthouse Cat

Illustrated by: Nathan Szerdy

Written by: Stephanie Szerdy

Printing by: Ponce de Leon Inlet Lighthouse Preservation Association, Inc.

For information please go to
nathanszerdy.com

Dedicated to:

The group of concerned citizens who came together in 1972 to form the Ponce de Leon Inlet Lighthouse Preservation Association, and to all those who have worked so diligently to restore, manage, and interpret this historic site.

Once teetering on the brink of destruction, the Ponce de Leon Inlet Lighthouse now exists as one of the finest and best preserved light stations in America. It stands today as one of the few stations in the country to have earned the prestigious designation as a National Historic Landmark.

The Preservation Association operates as a 501 (c)(3) nonprofit organization. Funding for all ongoing restoration, maintenance, and educational projects is generated through admission and gift shop sales, memberships, and private/corporation donations. Originally managed by an all-volunteer grass-roots association, the specialized skills required to properly preserve and operate the Ponce de Leon Inlet Lighthouse necessitated the transformation of the Preservation Association into the professional museum organization that exists today.

To learn more about the unique history of the Ponce de Leon Inlet Light Station and ways to support the Association's ongoing efforts to preserve this National Historic Landmark, please visit our website at

www.PonceInlet.org

Ponce de Leon Inlet Lighthouse Preservation Association, Inc.

4931 South Peninsula Drive, Ponce Inlet, FL. 32127

Phone: (386) 761-1821 * Fax: (386) 761-3121

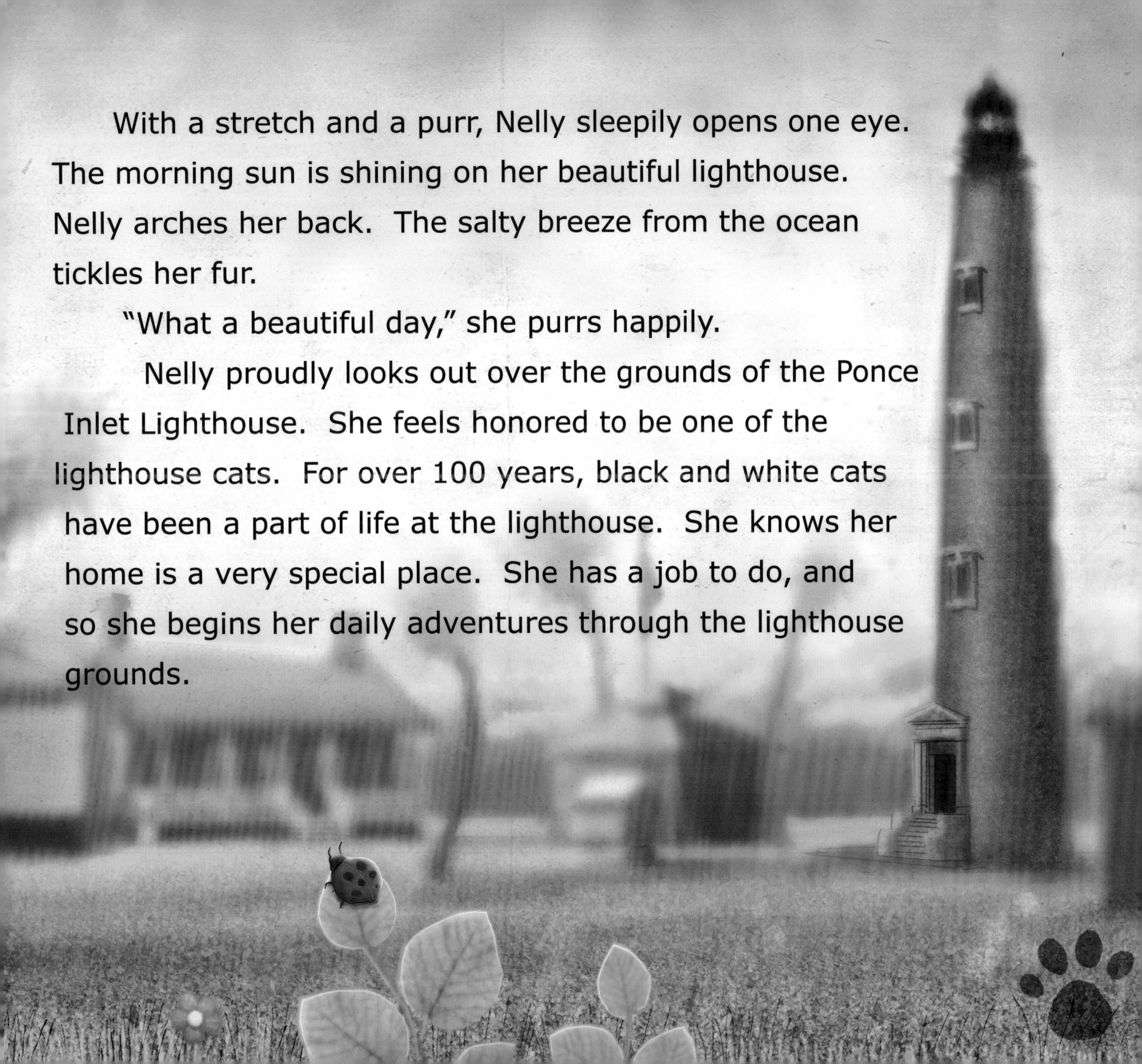

With a stretch and a purr, Nelly sleepily opens one eye. The morning sun is shining on her beautiful lighthouse. Nelly arches her back. The salty breeze from the ocean tickles her fur.

"What a beautiful day," she purrs happily.

Nelly proudly looks out over the grounds of the Ponce Inlet Lighthouse. She feels honored to be one of the lighthouse cats. For over 100 years, black and white cats have been a part of life at the lighthouse. She knows her home is a very special place. She has a job to do, and so she begins her daily adventures through the lighthouse grounds.

Nelly knows that her lighthouse is important because it serves as a guide for ships. When it is nighttime or stormy, sailors can see the shining beam of light from the tower, and they know that land is nearby. The light also marks the location where the rivers flow out into the sea. The sailors look for the light so they can find their way safely home.

Many years ago, families lived at the lighthouse. The fathers were the keepers and worked hard to keep the light shining brightly. The mothers and children lived and worked and played at the lighthouse. The families had cats, like Nelly, and the cats had jobs too.

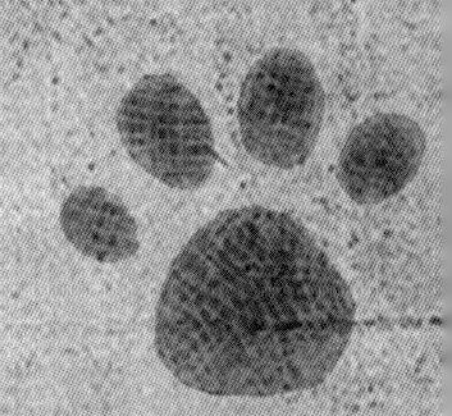

The job of the lighthouse cat is to make sure there are no pests at the lighthouse. Nelly's green eyes peer beneath the houses.

"Are you in there little mouse?" she hisses, "There will be no mice at my lighthouse!"

When the families lived at the lighthouse, the mice would steal the family's food. The cats kept the food safe by scaring the rodents away.

Lighthouse cats also protected the children by keeping away more dangerous creatures, like snakes. Nelly snoops and sniffs around the tower. Her eyes scan all around. "No snakes or mice today," she purrs to herself.

Nelly continues her journey around the lighthouse grounds. She knows that not all creatures are harmful. The lighthouse is home to some wonderful animals.

Nelly finds a large hole in the sand. She peers inside.

"Good morning Leon! Wake up!"

She hears a scuffle and a scratch inside, as Leon climbs out of his hole. His long neck stretches out of his shell and he blinks his old wrinkly eyes.

Leon is a gopher tortoise, a very rare type of reptile. He makes his home underground, but he still loves to bask in the warm Florida sun.

"You are missing some beautiful sunshine," she says.

Leon yawns. "Thanks Nelly, this really warms up my old shell."

Nelly looks up as a large shadow passes overhead. It is a pelican soaring on the ocean breeze.

"Hello there!" calls Nelly from far below.

Willy circles around to get a better look at her.

"Please tell me what you can see so high up in the sky!" Nelly calls. "Is it beautiful? Can you see my tower?"

"Of course I can see your tower, little cat! It's the tallest thing around!" replies Willy.

"Tell me more! What else do you see?"

"I see the three rivers. Your tower marks the spot where they all meet. They all flow together into the big ocean. That's where I'm going now. There are lots of tasty fish in the ocean! It's breakfast time!"

Thinking of fish, Nelly licks her lips as she watches Willy soar away to find his meal.

Nelly continues to explore the grounds of the lighthouse. She creeps quietly along the nature trail into the palm forest.

She can see something moving behind a palmetto tree. It is a very strange creature. He is very busy digging around in the sand for worms and insects.

Nelly tiptoes behind him. She gives him a big... playful... pounce!

Rowli snorts with shock and curls into a tight little ball. Nelly falls in the grass, laughing.

"Aw, come out Rowli! It's just me!" Nelly giggles.

"Nelly! What a surprise!" says the armadillo as he uncurls. "What are you doing here?"

"I want to hear more stories! Please tell me what you have seen!" Nelly listens to Rowli's stories of adventure. He tells her how he roams far into the forest looking for food, but he never gets lost. He always looks to Nelly's tower to find his way home.

Nelly loves her home. She happily walks along the brick paths around the lighthouse.

She chases the butterflies and dragonflies, although she is never quite quick enough to catch them. She stares at the fancy lizards that run across the sidewalks. She gazes at the hopping, singing tree frogs.

She watches bugs, lizards, and frogs all day, but the visitors are her favorite thing to watch.

In the past, the lighthouse was home to the workers and their families, but now the lighthouse is open to everyone. Visitors come from all over the world to see Nelly's wonderful red tower.

Nelly greets them as they walk onto the grounds. "Welcome to my lighthouse!" she purrs as she rubs against their legs.

She watches as they disappear into the tower. She waits, and waits, and waits...while they climb up, up, up... all 203 steps. Then they reappear at the top of the tower and peer over the railings down to the ground. They look very small up there, so high above Nelly.

"I wonder what they can see..." Nelly imagines what the ocean and the rivers look like 175 feet above the ground.

"That must be what the birds see," she decides.

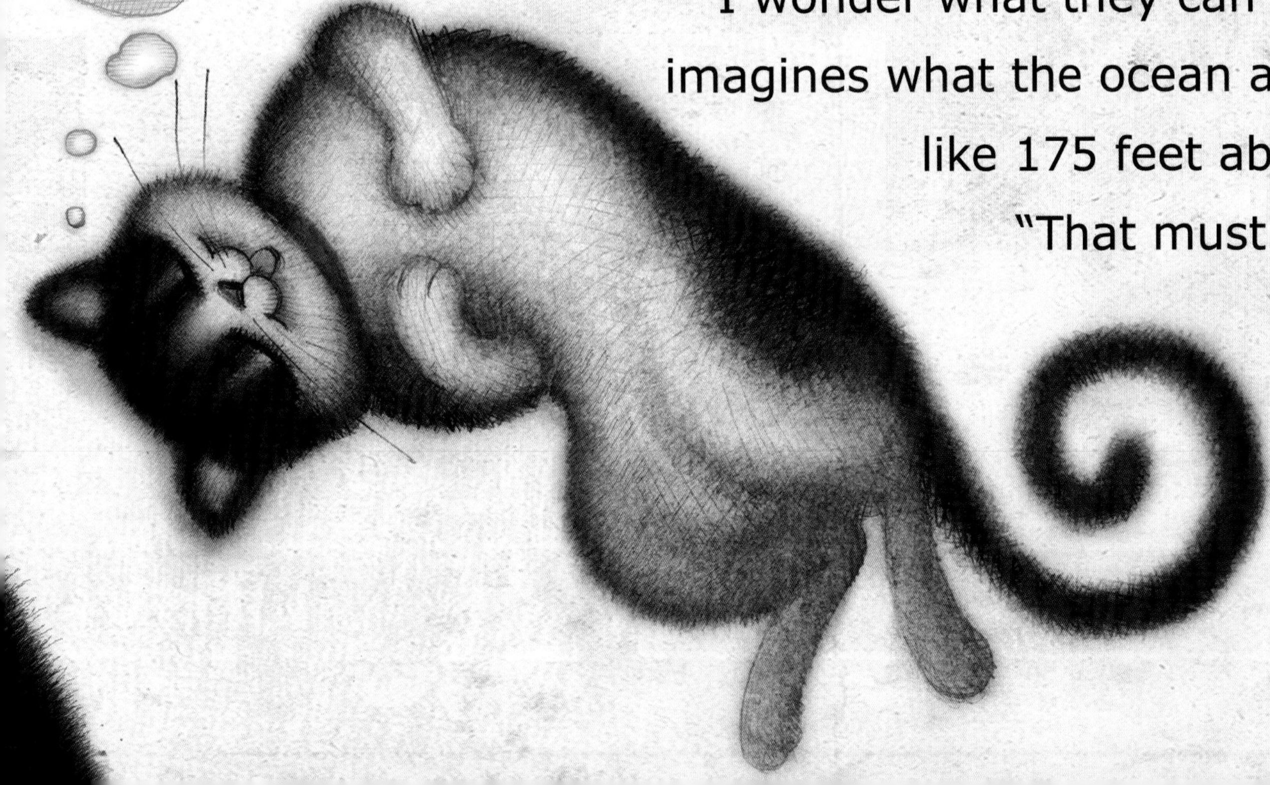

Nelly enjoys seeing all of the people. They are always different. Tall people and short people. Young people and old people. People who speak many languages. Sometimes they come in beautiful, shiny antique cars. Sometimes they come on roaring motorcycles.

She watches them take photographs. She purrs when they pet her. She plays in the grass with the children. Many of the visitors come back year after year. No matter where the people come from, they always love Nelly, and they love her lighthouse.

After a very busy day, the sun is beginning to set over the marshes. Usually, this is when the visitors start to go home, but today is different. Instead of people leaving the lighthouse, more and more people are coming in. They seem excited!

Nelly is very curious. She quietly follows the people to see where they are going. All of the people are climbing the tower. They gather at the top, facing the south.

"What can they possibly be looking at?" Nelly thinks.

The sky is getting darker and darker, but the people are still waiting. Nelly stretches her neck and tries to find what the people are looking for.

Suddenly, a beautiful orange glow lights the night sky. It is like a sunrise! Nelly's eyes widen with surprise.

"It can't be morning! What can this be?" she wonders.

The orange light grows bigger and bigger. Then she sees it. The space shuttle is rising into the sky! It is followed by a tail of beautiful fire. The amazing glowing path of light and smoke curve toward the ocean. Nelly's green eyes watch the light grow smaller and smaller, until it finally disappears into the starry night sky.

Nelly hears the visitors on top of the tower. She turns her ears to listen to their cheers and applause. Now she knows why so many people came to her tower so late at night. It was more magnificent than anything she had ever seen.

After the excitement of the shuttle launch, the people come down from the tower one-by-one.

"Goodnight!" Nelly meows, as the visitors wave to each other, and make their way home. A few of them stop to give Nelly a goodbye scratch behind her ears. After all the people are gone, the grounds are very quiet. Nelly listens carefully. The only sounds in the air are the distant crashing of the waves and the chirping of insects.

As she thinks about her exciting day, Nelly looks up at the stars and the moon. A long beam of light stretches out from the top of the lighthouse and reaches far into the darkness. Nelly wonders if sailors out on the dark ocean are looking for her tower. She happily curls up and watches the spinning light, as she dreams of more adventures at the Ponce Inlet Lighthouse.

Ponce de Leon Inlet

The lighthouse is 175 feet tall. It is the TALLEST lighthouse in Florida.

It was first opened in 1887.

The lighthouse and the town of Ponce Inlet are named for the Spanish explorer, Ponce de Leon, who explored Florida's coast in 1513.

The lighthouse is made of over one million bricks.

After many years of restoration, the lighthouse became a National Historic Landmark in 1998.

The inside of the lighthouse has a spiral staircase. It takes over 200 steps to reach the top!

Light Station

The light at the top flashes 6 times every 30 seconds. It can be seen over 18 miles away.

The first lighthouse in the area was built in 1835 but fell over a year later in a big storm!

The first lighthouse keeper was William Rowlinski. In the story, Willy the pelican and Rowli the armadillo are named for him.

Nelly is named after the Fresnel lens.

Meet the Author
Stephanie Szerdy

Stephanie grew up with a love of language and stories. She is a middle school teacher specializing in science and English. Stephanie feels a deep connection with the coastal environment. She enjoys SCUBA diving and learning about marine life. She finds inspiration in the beauty and rich history of Florida's coast, where she lives with her husband, Nathan.

Meet the Artis
Nathan Szerd

Nathan's imagination home to a cast of whimsic characters. He brings the dreams to life through h illustrations. His artwo has appeared in a variet of forms includir caricatures, mural computer software, an museum exhibit desigr He is currently creating series of children's book and writing his own graphic novel

Please visit www.NathanSzerdy.com for more!

Thanks to Judy J. DiCarlo & Carson J. Domey for all their efforts in developing this project.